"HI! I'M **HATCH** I'M A BABY LEATHERBACK!"

All over the world, mummy turtles
have a special time and place where they
go to lay eggs with their little babies inside.

OUR MUMMY CARRIED US IN HER TUMMY ON A TRIP SOUTH...

NORTH AMERICA

CARIBBEAN

SOUTH AMERICA

REALLY FAR

X

EVEN
FURTHER

X

She swam thousands of miles.

HERE

X

ON A MOONLIT NIGHT

Until she arrived at a beautiful beach
in the Caribbean!

Mummy searched the beach
looking for somewhere
cozy for us...

"UNDER THE TREES BY THE RIVER LOOKS SAFE."

she thought.

...She thought she had found
the perfect spot!

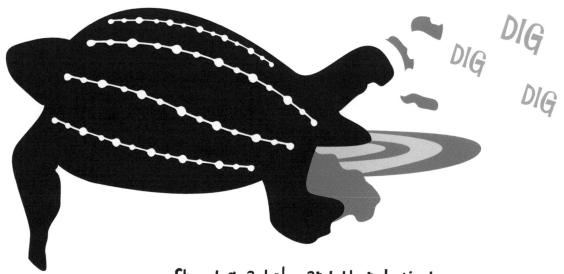

She dug a hole and then buried
us in our eggs, deep in the sand.

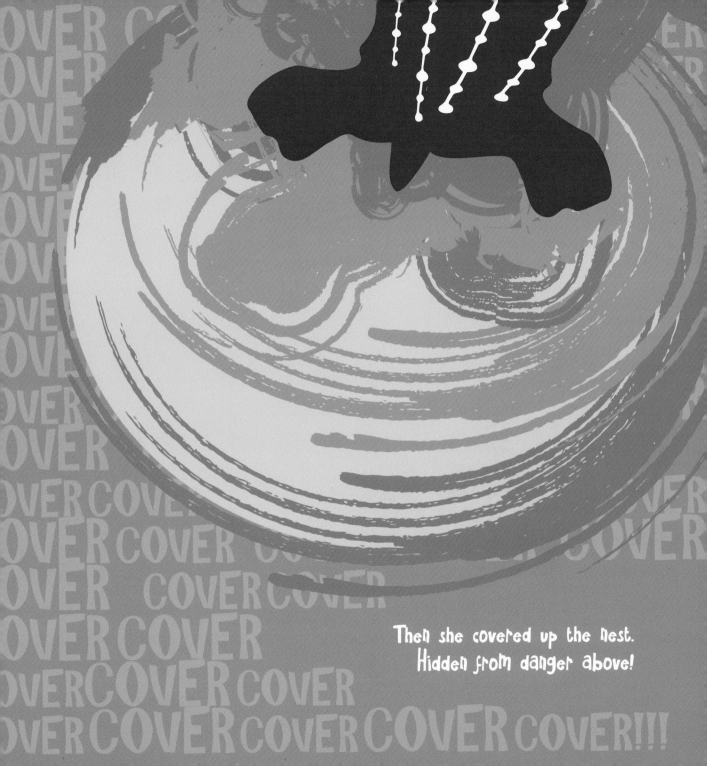

Then she covered up the nest.
Hidden from danger above!

COVER COVER COVER OVER OVER OVER OVER OVER OVER OVER OVER OVER OVER OVER COVER OVER COVER COVER OVER COVER COVER COVER COVER COVER COVER COVER OVER COVER COVER COVER COVER!!!

Mummy headed back out to the sea
leaving us behind in our nest.

2 MONTHS LATER

It was time to get to the sea!

Our race was **oh!**

RUMBLE RUMBLE RUMBLE RUMBLE
RUMBLE RUMBLE RUMBLE RUMBLE RUMBLE

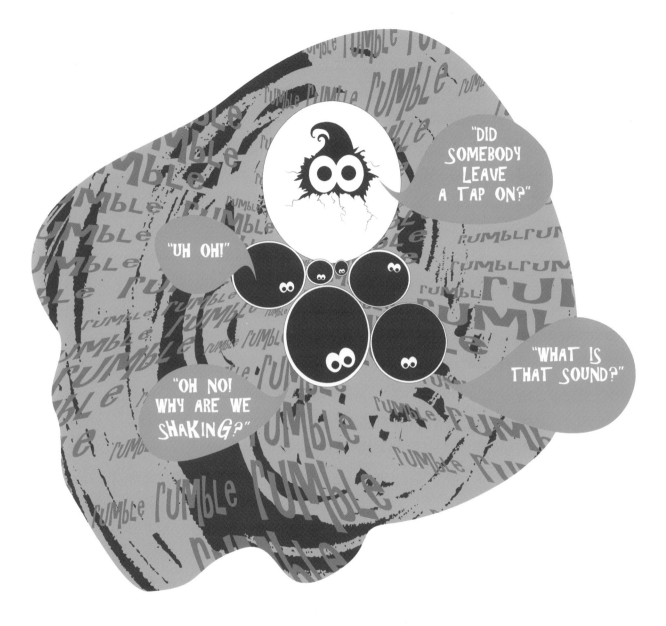

There was a **strange** noise outside. It sounded like water!

No! No! No! The river had broken its banks!!!

The water was coming in fast!
I HAD to hurry so I could win the race!

Woohoo!! I was in front!

I was out first!!!

wait...

wait...

wait!

NOooooooooOoooooooooooOoooooooooooo

SLIPPING
SLIPPING
SLIPPING
SLIPPING
SLIPPING
SLIPPING
SLIPPING

The nest was filling up with water
I tried to climb out, but

the walls were crumbling!!!

JUMP

I climbed to the top.

CLIMB

CLIMB

CLIMB

JUMP

Then I jumped as high as I could.

But...

Then I had an idea!

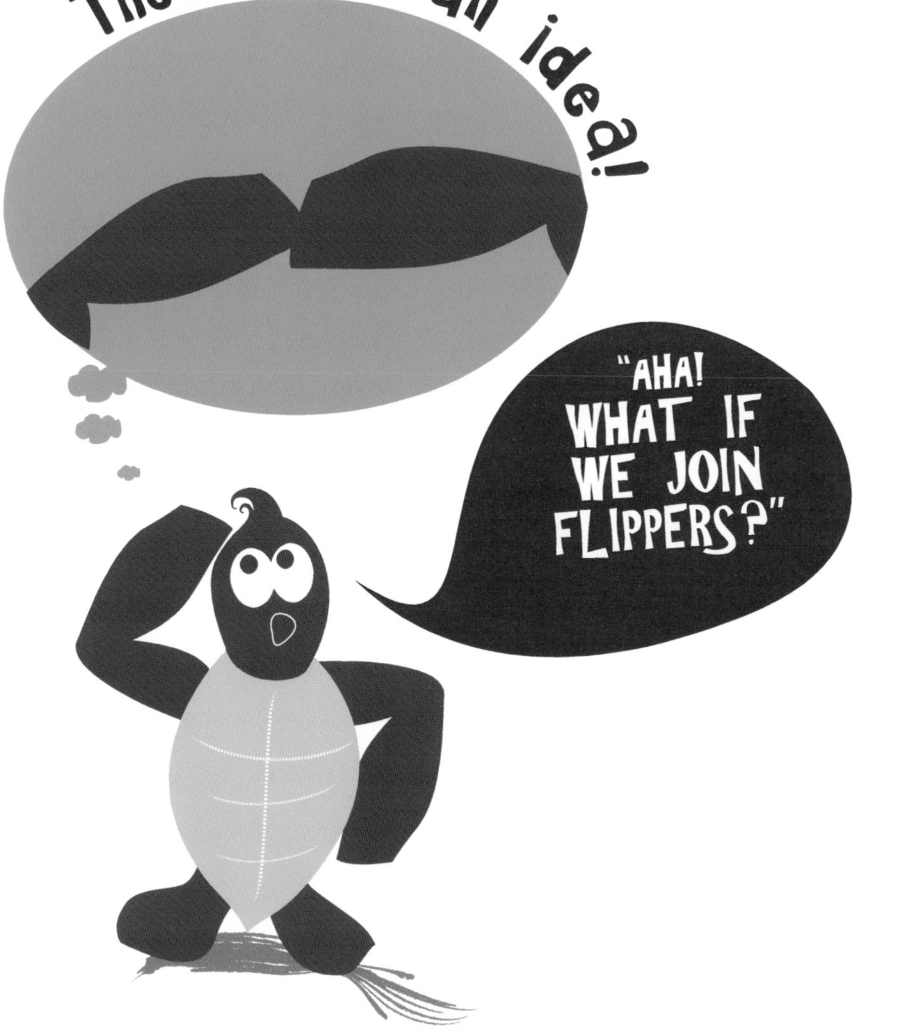

We grabbed each other's flippers
forming a chain.

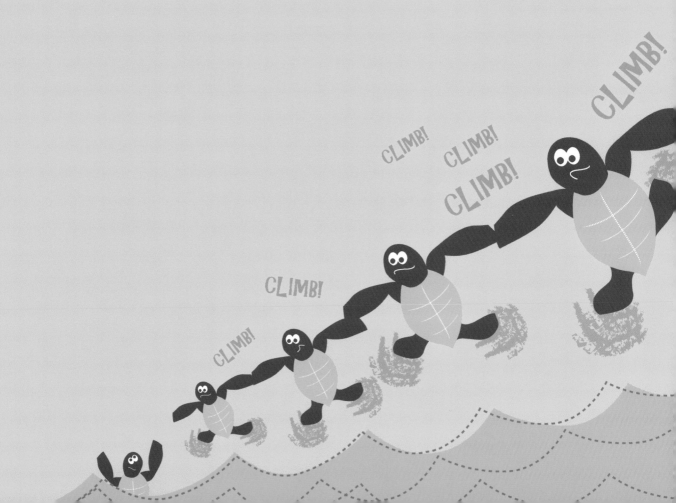

CLIMB! CLIMB!

Then we climbed on top of one another and...

...One by one, we all climbed out.

Just as we got to the surface,
The river crashed
right through our nest!

We scrambled across the sand
towards the sea.

I waited back for my brother and sister who needed a little help.

And finally.....

...Everyone
made it safely
to the sea!

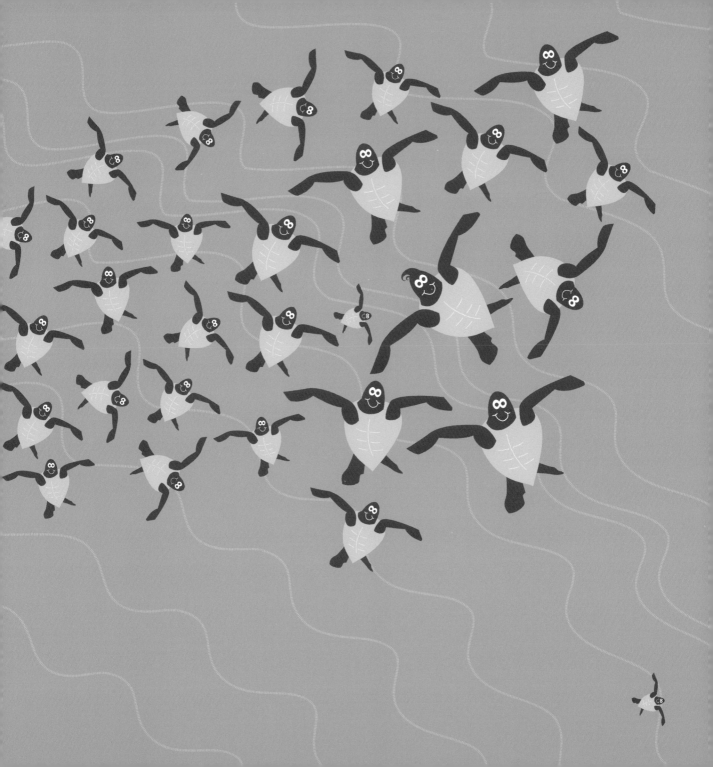

Inspired by Caribbean kiddies
scattered all over the world.
Miles apart, but forever
island babies at heart.

The Caribbean region supports one of the largest leatherback nesting populations worldwide, with an estimated 6,000 visiting its shores annually.

Leatherbacks like all sea turtles start out as eggs buried in sandy nests. The hatchlings face many predators as they scamper seaward.

It is estimated that only one in one thousand leatherback turtles survive to adulthood.

First edition 2014. Published by Everything Slight Pepper
P.O.. Box 1373 Wrightson Road, POS, Trinidad and Tobago

ISBN: 978-976-95350-0-80

Text & illustrations by Jeunanne Alkins
© 2014 Everything Slight Pepper

www.espjrisland.com

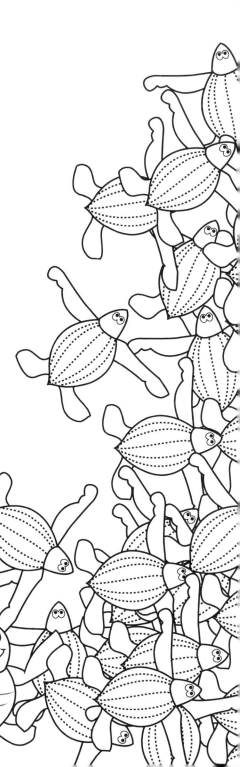
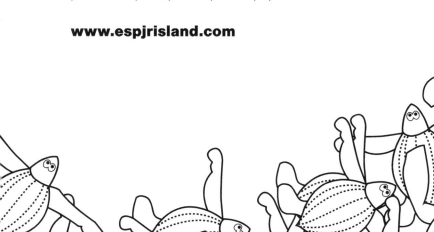

READY, SET...

HatcH!

Hatch is hiding!
Can you find him in this crowd?

CPSIA information can be obtained at www.ICGtesting.com
Printed in the USA
BVIW12n1924061117
499566BV00028B/200

* 9 7 8 9 7 6 9 5 3 5 0 0 8 *